MID-CONTINENT PUBLIC LIBRARY
15616 E. 24 HWY
INDEPENDENCE, MO 64050

3 0 0 0 4 0 0

D0430983

School Is A Nightmare #3

Shocktober

WITHDRAWN
FROM THE RECORDS OF THE
MID-CONTINENT PUBLIC LIBRARY

RAYMOND BEAN

Copyright © 2011 Raymond Bean
All rights reserved.

ISBN: 1478233842
ISBN 13: 9781478233848

www.raymondbcan.com

Raymond Bean books

Sweet Farts Series
Sweet Farts #1
Sweet Farts #2 Rippin' It Old School
Sweet Farts #3 Blown Away

School Is A Nightmare Series
School Is A Nightmare #1
First Week, Worst Week
School Is A Nightmare #2 The Field Trip
School Is A Nightmare #3 Shocktober
School Is A Nightmare #4 Yuck Mouth and the
Thanksgiving Miracle
School Is A Nightmare #5
(Coming Winter 2013)

For Stacy, Ethan, and Chloe.

Interested in scheduling an
author visit or web based author talk?
Email us at raymondbeanbooks@gmail.com

Contents

1. Shocktober   1

2. Halloween Party-less   7

3. Order It   11

4. What Will We Feed It To?   15

5. Mrs. Fiesta Is Awesome!   19

6. Myrtle On the Loose   25

7. Grounded   35

8. I'm Sorry I'm A Werewolf   39

9. I Have To What?   43

10. Where's the Blue Clone Trooper?   47

11. Payback Is a Blast   53

12. Nobody Move!   57

13. Think about It   63

14. Calamity   69

15. The Best Halloween Ever   73

16. Can I Trust You?   79

17. Don't Tell Mom and Dad   81

18. Calamity's Calamity   85

19. You Win   89

20. Simba, the Halloween Monster   91

1
Shocktober

The only thing October has going for it is Halloween. It's like some kind of a joke that Halloween is always on the very last day of the month. You have to wait thirty long days before you get to put on your costume and collect all the free candy. It's just not fair.

It amazes me that Halloween is one of the greatest days of the year, but they don't even close school for it. If I grow up to be president, I'll make Halloween a national holiday and close all the schools.

Actually, Halloween is so awesome kids should get two days off for it. We should get one day to trick-or-treat and the next day to eat candy in peace or to recover from eating too much candy the night before. Unfortunately, I'm not the president yet, so a national holiday in honor of candy is not going to happen anytime soon.

Another awesome thing about Halloween is dressing up. I've never really had the chance to wear a cool Halloween costume before because up until this year, my mom basically picked my costume. It's so lame. Every year my sisters are the ones who choose what I'm going to be. Mom always says she's going to let me pick, but then my sisters come up with an idea that involves me. They like to wear what they call a "group costume." My mom always falls in love with their idea, and *bam*, that's the costume. For example, in second grade, Becky and Mindy thought it was a great idea for Becky to be Cinderella,

Mindy to be the wicked stepmother, and for me to dress up as the prince.

I totally didn't want to be the prince, but once they told Mom, she fell in love with the idea. I was Prince Charming. There was nothing I could do. It was terrible. To this day, some of my friends still call me Prince Charming.

Last year, in third grade, Becky wanted to be Dorothy from *The Wizard of Oz*, Mindy wanted to be the Wicked Witch of the North (which was actually perfect for her), and I had to dress up as Toto the dog! Again I complained, but my mom thought it was even cuter than Prince Charming, so I was Toto the dog.

This year I really made my case to Mom, and she agreed to let me have an "independent" costume, even though she really wished I'd think about a costume with the girls.

"I want to be a Clone Trooper," I told her.

"You can get it if you order it with your own money," she told me.

The girls tried to convince me to be a part of their costume again, but I told them there was no way. Unless they wanted to be my prisoners, I wasn't interested.

"Come on, Justin," Mindy said.

"We're going to make our costumes this year. They will be the best costumes in the whole school," Becky added.

"I'm going to be a Clone Trooper. If you guys want to be some kind of horrible space creatures that I've arrested to return to the emperor, that would be awesome. Anything else, you can count me out," I said.

"You can help make your costume too," Mindy said.

"No, thanks. I'm ordering my costume online. Mom said we can order it tonight after dinner."

"Don't you want to know what we're going to be?" Becky asked.

"Nope."

"We're going to be Sarabi and Mufasa," Mindy said.

"I don't know what that means."

"They're the mother and father in *The Lion King*," Becky explained.

"We want you to be Simba!" they both said at the same time.

"There's no way I'm dressing up as a baby lion cub."

"Oh, you'd be the cutest little lion king there's ever been!" Mom said, clearly pushing for the Simba costume.

"I'm not dressing up as a baby lion. I'm going to be a Clone Trooper. This year, I'm not going to be cute!"

2
Halloween Party-less

It's been pretty clear since the first day of school that my teacher, Mrs. Cliff, doesn't like me very much. I did manage to get on her good side at the end of our first field trip. The trip was a complete nightmare, but I met pop sensation Jason Freeber and introduced him to Mrs. Cliff, who's a huge fan. She treated me like gold the whole next week, but it didn't last.

After they met, Jason's assistant emailed a picture of him with his arm around Mrs. Cliff backstage. She framed it and kept it on her desk.

Unfortunately, she'd emailed him a few more times and hadn't heard from him again. It was nice while it lasted, but Mrs. Cliff's good mood vanished as fast as it had arrived. Before I knew it, I was back in the doghouse.

On the first Monday of October, it was raining really hard. Mrs. Cliff is always extra cranky on rainy days. Of course, she called on me right after the morning announcements.

"Justin, what Halloween topic are you going to research for our project?" Mrs. Cliff asked.

"I'm still not sure," I admitted.

"You're aware that topics are due today?"

"I know, but I couldn't decide. Can't I have one more day?"

"No, you already had two weeks to prepare. You know my policy—five points off for every day it's late. It doesn't even have to be complete. Just let us know what your topic is. I hope you have it ready for tomorrow."

In the middle of September, Mrs. Cliff had assigned us a research project on a Halloween topic. We were allowed to select any topic at all as long as it had a connection to Halloween. Some kids were studying the history of vampires, some zombies, and others were studying witches. A few kids decided to focus more on the whole history of the holiday. I was the only kid who didn't bring my idea in on time. I also had no idea what I was going to research. I don't mind reading about Halloween creatures, but I definitely don't want to have to write about them.

I raised my hand. "Mrs. Cliff, are we going to have a Halloween party?"

"Justin, you can't raise your hand and immediately start talking. Please don't interrupt like that."

"Sorry," I said. "I'm just curious about our party. My friend Aaron in Mrs. Fiesta's class said they're having a party on Halloween day."

"I'm aware that Mrs. Fiesta's class is having a party, but we will be doing something even more exciting. We'll be having a research share!" she said, as if all the kids would be excited about not having a party and sharing our research instead. The room fell silent.

I raised my hand and waited this time.

"Yes, Justin," she said.

"Can't we do the research share *and* a party?"

"I'm afraid not. We'll have a great time sharing our research on Halloween, though. I can't wait to hear what you've all written."

I couldn't believe my bad luck. Halloween was coming, and I was party-less.

3
Order It

That night, Becky and Mindy worked at the kitchen table on their costumes. They had *The Lion King* soundtrack on in the background. It was so loud I could hardly think while I finished my homework. I had to come up with a topic for my research report. I went on the Internet and searched *Halloween monsters*.

I decided to do my project on werewolves, since I was pretty sure Mrs. Cliff was actually capable of becoming one. In the article I read, it said werewolves could paralyze young children simply by gazing at them. It also said they have curled nails and walk with a bit of a hunch. It was pretty clear to me that Mrs. Cliff was probably a werewolf.

I had just finished filling out my research report paper for Mrs. Cliff when Mom sat next to me.

"Why don't we go online and order your costume?" she said.

"That's a great idea," I said, putting the paper back in my folder.

"It's not too late to be Simba," Becky reminded me.

"*Hakuna matata*," Mindy said.

"I told you, I'm not going to be cute this year. I'm going to be a Clone Trooper."

"Here it is," Mom said, pointing to the screen.

"That's not the one I want. I want the blue one with the real helmet. Dad said I could get it." We clicked around a little more and soon discovered that most of the Clone Trooper costumes were kind of lame-looking. Finally we found one that looked awesome. "That's it!" I said, excited.

"That looks great," Mom said, "but I don't recognize the company selling it. We should stick with a company we know so we don't have any problems with it getting here on time."

"Please, Mom! That's the one. It looks like the ones right out of the movie! The other ones look like they're made out of garbage bags."

"I guess we can order it and return it if it's not good quality. It does look a little too good to be true, though. The price is less than the ones that you don't like."

"It must be a sale. Come on, Mom. Please order it."

"You're sure you don't want to be Simba?" Mom asked one last time.

"I absolutely don't want to be Simba, and I think I've earned this costume after being what the girls wanted me to be all these years."

"Okay," she said. "Let's just hope it's good quality."

"It will be," I said. "This is going to be the best Halloween ever!"

4
What Will We Feed It To?

The rest of that week went by pretty slow. It rained every day, and we were stuck inside for recess. On Thursday, I walked into class to find an animal tank near Mrs. Cliff's desk.

"What's in the tank, Mrs. Cliff?" I asked.

"Please place your things in the cubby and get going on your morning work, Justin," she said.

"But I just want to know what's in the tank."

"And I'm asking you to have a seat. But if you must know, the question is not what is in the tank, but what *will be* in the tank later today."

I put my stuff away and got to work. I could hardly concentrate. It was driving me crazy.

After lunch, Mrs. Cliff taught us a lesson on mammals. Then she asked us to guess what mammal we thought would go in the tank.

Adam Lint raised his hand first. "A bird."

"Birds aren't mammals," I interrupted.

"You're correct, Justin, but please refrain from interrupting your peers."

I felt a little embarrassed and annoyed. You would think she'd appreciate the help. That's one of the problems with Mrs. Cliff. She has so many rules that I feel like I can't be myself. I wasn't trying to be rude or obnoxious. I was just trying to help out. Sure, I should have raised my hand, but when in life do you have to raise your hand other than in a class? It doesn't seem like good practice for the real world.

Finally, Cynthia Murt guessed a mouse. Half the class said, "Eewwww," and the other half thought it was cool.

"You're right, Cynthia," said Mrs. Cliff. "We'll be taking care of a little mouse named Myrtle. She is a special mouse, and over the course of the next few weeks, you'll learn what makes her *so* special."

"What are we going to feed her to?" I asked.

Mrs. Cliff looked horrified. "We're not feeding her to anything. Why would you say something like that?"

"I feed mice to my snakes all the time," I said. "I have a boa constrictor named Mr. Squeeze and a big garter snake that I found in the woods by my house. His name is Stanky. I named him that—"

Mrs. Cliff interrupted. "Justin, you're interrupting again. I'm sure your snakes are very interesting, but we aren't talking about them right now. We're talking about our new mouse named Myrtle, and we won't be feeding her to anyone." She lifted a small cardboard box from behind her desk. "Myrtle is in this container. It will be our job to take care of her. Let's break up into groups and decide what we'll need and how we're going to split up the duties of taking care of her."

5
Mrs. Fiesta Is Awesome!

On the bus ride home, Aaron told me all about the cool things Mrs. Fiesta had planned for Halloween in his class.

"It's going to be the best day ever," he said. "We're having all kinds of candy and stuff. Mrs. Fiesta is famous for making a bunch of gross stuff to touch, like a box of brains and a bag of intestines! Man, I can't wait."

"It's not fair," I said. "It should be the same for every class. I can't believe you're going to have the best day ever, and I'm going to be a few doors away listening to a bunch of research reports."

"That's pretty bad," he admitted. "Mrs. Cliff is really ripping you guys off."

I was quiet the rest of the ride home. It wasn't fair. It made me not even want to go to her class anymore. When I got off the bus, I found Mom waiting to drive me home because the rain was pretty heavy.

"What's wrong?" she asked.

"I can't stand Mrs. Cliff."

"Oh, come on. She can't be that bad. The woman has been teaching there since Dad was in elementary school."

"I know. That's probably part of the problem. She's, like, a thousand years old and has no idea how to have fun anymore."

"That's not nice," Mom said.

"I mean it. Mrs. Fiesta's class is planning this awesome party for Halloween with candy and scary stuff, and you know what we're doing?"

"What?"

"We're writing reports all month and sharing them on Halloween!"

"That sounds interesting," Mom said.

"Halloween isn't supposed to be interesting. It's supposed to be fun! Research reports aren't fun. Can't you call the principal and tell him you want me moved to Mrs. Fiesta's class?"

"That's not how it works, and you know it. You'll have plenty of time to have fun on Halloween after you get home from school. It will be fun. You'll see."

"I don't know. I'm not counting on it."

When I got home, I went upstairs to feed Mr. Squeeze and Stanky. I'd almost lost Mr. Squeeze a few weeks ago, when he got out of his tank and scared my sister half to death. My parents were going to take him away, but they changed their minds and let me keep him as long as I was more careful with him. I'd found Stanky in the woods and convinced my parents to let me keep him too.

I opened my huge closet, which is where I keep their tanks, and walked in. I had emptied all my clothes out of the closet so I could keep the tanks and a few heat lamps in there. Mom says it's a waste of a walk-in closet, but it's the perfect place for them because even if they get out of the tanks, they're probably not going to get out of my closet. I hadn't mentioned it to Mom or Dad, but Mr. Squeeze was getting very powerful, and I was having a hard time keeping him in his tank. He'd managed to get out of his tank a few times, but never out of the closet.

The snakes love it when I let them out of the tanks and move around in the closet. They're probably the luckiest snakes in the world because I snuck in a few branches and large stones from outside, which I set up to make them feel like they're outside.

Becky opened the closet door and yelled when she saw the snakes out of the tanks.

"Quiet!" I insisted.

"You can't have them out of the tanks!" she said.

"I know I'm not supposed to, but they're getting really big. I have to give them time to move around."

"Mom and Dad would totally not approve."

"Let's not get in an argument about it, Becky. I've got to let them out, but I'm being safe."

"Mom and Dad told you specifically to leave them in their tanks because they scare me and Mindy, and I think Dad too."

"I don't know what to tell you. This is safe."

"Mom!" Becky shouted.

Becky told Mom and Dad, and they grounded me for the weekend.

"What were you thinking?" Mom asked.

"I thought it would be safe because they're in the tank and in the closet. If they get out of the tank, they'll still be stuck in the closet."

"That wasn't the deal. The deal was that you would keep them in their tanks and not take them out without our permission. I don't mind if you keep the tanks in your closet, but you cannot take them out of the tanks," Dad said.

"Fine," I agreed, shooting Becky a look.

6
Myrtle On the Loose

I had to give the girls credit. They were really putting a ton of work into their costumes. They seemed to spend every free minute working at the kitchen table. The costumes didn't look like anything yet, but I was happy the project was keeping them busy. It felt like I had the house to myself.

I left for school on Friday, excited for the three-day Columbus Day weekend, and sad that I would be grounded for the entire time. I almost asked Mom if my grounding included Monday, but figured I should wait until after school.

At recess, I watched Myrtle. Rain was pouring down outside, and we were stuck inside for the fifth day in a row. She was sleeping in the corner of the tank.

Cameron, who doesn't usually say much, sat down next to me and said, "That thing never does anything."

"I know," I said. "It seems to sleep most of the time."

"Too bad Mrs. Cliff didn't get us something cool for the class pet, like a bird."

"Really? You'd want a pet bird?"

"Yeah, I have like seven of them at home. They're cool."

"I never had a bird as a pet, but my mom says they're dirty and noisy. That's why she agreed to get me a snake."

"Snakes are terrible pets," Cameron said.

"No, they're not!" I exclaimed. "Snakes are awesome. They're easy to take care of, they don't make noise, and they're cool to hold."

"And they can kill you."

"You sound like one of my sisters. I have a boa constrictor and a garter snake. They aren't poisonous. They eat mice like Miss Myrtle."

"I dare you to pick Myrtle up," Cameron said.

I was kind of surprised at the dare because he always seemed like such a well-behaved kid. I knew it wasn't the right thing to do, but I'd held a zillion mice before, so I said, "What will you give me?"

"I'll give you five bucks," he said.

"Nah, it's not worth the risk. If Mrs. Cliff finds out, I'll get in major trouble."

"I'll be right back," he said and walked over to his friend Mark. The two of them talked for a few seconds, and then he went over to Karen and May. Karen and May went to several other kids in the class. Finally, Cameron came back and sat in his seat next to me. "I'll give you five bucks, and everyone else in the class will give you a dollar. That adds up to thirty bucks."

It was too tempting to resist. "Now we have a deal," I said.

"You've got to take Myrtle out of the cage and hold her for at least a minute," he added.

"A minute is a long time to have her out without getting caught." I pointed to our recess monitor, Mrs. Curtis, who was sitting at a table on the far side of the class, near the door. "Thirty seconds," I said.

"Deal," Cameron said, putting his hand out for me to shake.

I couldn't help thinking that Cameron would make a good businessman one day. All he was missing was the suit and an office. "And everyone has to be quiet and not make noises that will get me in trouble."

Cameron signaled to Mark, and Mark walked over to Mrs. Curtis and started up a conversation with her. He stood so she couldn't see me or Myrtle's tank.

"Go ahead," Cameron said. "The clock starts when you get her out of the tank."

I quickly pulled the lid off the tank and slowly reached in to grab Myrtle. She looked a lot like the mice I feed to the snakes, but she was prettier, if a mouse can be considered pretty. She was sleeping, which made her easy to pick up. I took her out and held her carefully in my hands.

Karen walked over for a closer look. "Don't drop her," she whispered.

"I won't. I handle these little guys all the time."

"Ew," May said. "They're totally gross. I wouldn't touch that thing for all the money in the world."

"It's nothing," I said, feeling like the money was as good as mine.

"Fifteen seconds to go," Cameron said.

I looked over toward Mrs. Curtis to make sure Mark was still keeping her busy, and that's when a boom of thunder rocked the room like a bomb. I was so startled by it that I shrieked so loud they probably heard me on the space shuttle, and I dropped Myrtle.

"Get her!" Karen insisted.

I dropped to my knees to pick Myrtle up, but she scurried over May's foot. May screamed so loud that if I had long hair, it would have blown back. Myrtle was there one second and gone the next.

Mrs. Curtis appeared immediately. How she made it across the room in an instant was a complete mystery to me. "What's going on?" she demanded.

"Justin let Myrtle out of her tank," May said.

Mrs. Curtis looked in the tank and glared at me. "Mrs. Cliff made it crystal clear that no one was to open that tank for any reason. What does it say on the side of the tank?"

I stood to read what she was pointing at. Taped to the side of the tank was a sign I hadn't seen before. I read, "No one is to open this tank for any reason!" She had me. "I guess I didn't see that," I said, trying to look as cute as possible. It wasn't working. I could have looked cuter than a baby sea lion and it wouldn't have made a difference. Mrs. Curtis was furious.

"Find it!" she ordered.

"I will! I'm sorry, Mrs. Curtis." I was so nervous. I couldn't believe I'd dropped Myrtle. "Come on," I said to Cameron. "Help me out."

"No way! Mice give me the creeps."

Unbelievable, I thought. "Fine! I'll find it myself."

I dropped back to the floor. I knew mice liked small places, so I started looking behind the bookshelves. She'd probably gone in that direction first. As I crawled around on my hands and knees like an animal, the other kids learned what was going on, and the room instantly got very loud. Kids were laughing, screaming, and some were even helping me. It was so incredibly loud. Mrs. Curtis lost complete control of the class. She tried shouting for everyone to be quiet, but the noise didn't let up. That's when Mrs. Cliff got back from her lunch. The room fell silent the second she entered. It was like a magic trick the way she made the sound vanish. People instantly scrambled to their desks or started cleaning up their areas.

"Mrs. Curtis, may I speak with you in the hall, please?" she said.

The two women walked into the hall for a few minutes. I stayed on the floor and continued my search, but Myrtle was gone for good. "You still owe me thirty bucks," I whispered to Cameron.

"No way!" he whispered back. "You had her in your hand for about fifteen seconds. You lost the bet."

I'm going to get in so much trouble, I thought. Mrs. Cliff returned, looking angrier than ever. I wanted to crack a joke but figured it was too soon, and she'd get even more furious with me.

"Everyone kindly return to your seat," she said. "Justin, may I speak to you in the hall, please?"

I thought about making a run for it. I'd been in trouble at school before, but this felt like it was going to be a really big deal. I met her in the hallway, and she didn't say anything, which is sometimes the worst. When an adult just looks at you without talking when they're mad, it's a bad sign.

Finally she said, "You were well aware you shouldn't mess with Myrtle, but you took her out anyway."

"I'm sorry," I admitted. "Cameron dared me to take her out."

"If he dared you to jump off a bridge, would you do that too?"

"No," I said. My mom loved using that expression too. *There's a big difference between taking a mouse out of a tank and jumping off a bridge*, I thought, but didn't dare say that to Mrs. Cliff.

"I didn't mean to let her go. I was so startled when I heard the thunder that I dropped her. I tried to find her, but I think she got into or behind something. She'll come out later, when we quiet down."

"That won't do me any good, though, Justin. I need that mouse back in the tank now, and I'm guessing, with all that noise, she's hiding somewhere really safe and hard to find. I don't think she'll come out until after she has the babies."

"Babies?"

"Yep, Myrtle is pregnant. She'll probably have the babies this weekend."

7
Grounded

That night, Mom and Dad were super angry with me. Mrs. Cliff and the principal both called home. Mom and Dad had to pay to have a pest-removal expert visit the classroom and try to remove Myrtle safely. He couldn't find Myrtle, and the school and Mrs. Cliff didn't want to do anything to harm her or the babies, so they left her alone, wherever she was. Mrs. Cliff told Mom and Dad I'd learn my punishment on Tuesday, after Columbus Day weekend. She wanted some time to think it over.

"What were you thinking?" Dad asked at dinner.

"It was only supposed to be for thirty seconds," I said.

"Well, that didn't go as planned, did it?" Mom asked, clearly about to go off on me. "That mouse is a living thing, and it doesn't even belong to you. What made you think it would be okay to take it out of the tank in a class of twenty-five kids?"

"I don't know. I guess I just got carried away."

"You always get carried away," Becky added.

"Mind your business," I said.

"I think you had better stop talking before you're grounded straight through Halloween," Mom said.

"You wouldn't ground me on Halloween!"

"It might teach you the lesson you need to learn," Mindy said.

"Mind your business, Mindy," Mom warned.

"I just said the exact same thing to her and got in trouble! How come—"

"You are her brother. I'm her mother, and I'm warning you that you are way out on *very* thin ice. Step carefully, young man."

When Mom calls me "young man," it's never a good thing.

The girls were both enjoying the Myrtle situation. They sat at the table taking slow, little bites of their food, watching me get in trouble as if it were a play being put on for their enjoyment and they had front-row seats.

"Mrs. Cliff was really livid, and so was your principal," Dad said. "I want you to write an apology to each of them to go back to school on Monday."

"There's no school on Monday."

"On Tuesday then," Mom said.

"Am I grounded on Monday too?" I asked, knowing it was probably the wrong time to ask, but I couldn't resist.

"You're grounded until next Monday. I think a week spent at home reflecting on why it's important to respect other people's wishes and follow rules is in order," Mom said. "Mrs. Cliff also said you have a report due on Halloween. I want it done by Tuesday. You can work on it full-time over the holiday weekend. You have nothing else to do," Dad added.

"Can I play video games?" I asked.

"No!" Mindy and Becky said at the same time.

"Girls, mind your business," Dad said.

"Justin, you may not play video games, watch TV, or do any other activity that you enjoy. You're grounded," Mom said.

"I can't get the whole report done in a long weekend."

"Well, you'll have to. I suggest you get to work," Dad said.

8
I'm Sorry I'm A Werewolf

Monday night, I dreamed I'd turned into a werewolf. I was roaming the halls at school, terrifying the kids. The funny part was that even though I was a werewolf, I was still scared of Mrs. Cliff. Right before I woke, she had tracked me down and was yelling at me about how being a werewolf wasn't safe and I should be ashamed of myself.

I must have said, "I'm sorry I'm a werewolf" out loud because Mindy said, "You're such a weirdo."

"What are you doing in here?" I asked, slowly coming out of my werewolf dream.

"I was checking to make sure you have those snakes safely in their crates."

"They're called tanks, and they're safe in their tanks."

"Mom wants Becky and me to check them throughout the day to make sure you're keeping them safe like you promised."

Becky walked in and sat on my bed. "She doesn't trust you anymore," she said.

"It's a shame, too, because trust is the hardest thing to earn back," Mindy added.

"Can you guys get out of here?"

"Sure," Mindy said. "Breakfast is ready downstairs. You might want to eat up."

"It could be your last meal," Becky said. "I'm sure Mrs. Cliff has a pretty horrible punishment waiting for you."

I'd forgotten all about the fact that it was Tuesday and Mrs. Cliff was going to tell me my punishment. I immediately thought about what

I could do to make the punishment as little as possible. I imagined getting her flowers, but remembered she doesn't like flowers. Then I remembered that her favorite thing in the whole world is an apology. I sat down and wrote out the most sincere and lovely apology the world has ever seen. I put it in an envelope and drew a bunch of sea turtles (her favorite animal) on it. Then I rushed down for breakfast.

"You dreamed you were a werewolf?" my mother asked.

"I guess I did. I just remember Mrs. Cliff was chasing me."

"That's your guilt. You know that your behavior was monstrous and that your teacher shouldn't have to deal with such disrespect."

"I wrote her an apology," I said, holding it up.

Mom took it from me and inspected the note. "I'm impressed," she said. "Did your father help you write that?"

"Nope," I said.

"Good for you, Justin. That's nice of you."

"Does it mean I'm not grounded for so long?" I asked.

"Nice try," Mom said. "I don't care if you get the president to call her. You're grounded."

9
I Have To What?

Mrs. Cliff started the day on Tuesday by telling the kids, "Myrtle is still missing. I want you all to be very careful as you move about the room. If you see her, stay calm and tell me immediately. Also, she's pregnant, so we're hoping to get her before she has the babies or sneaks out of the school."

She didn't say anything about my punishment, and I didn't remind her. At one o'clock, when the class went to gym, she asked me to stay behind. "Sit down, Justin," she said.

"I made you an apology card," I said, hoping it would earn me an easier punishment.

"Thank you. I look forward to getting it."

"I'll go get it for you."

"You can get it later. I'd like to talk a bit more about what happened last Friday. You deliberately disobeyed a class rule and ended up putting our class pet and her babies in grave danger."

"I'm really sorry. It was a bad idea, but Cameron made me do it."

"It's upsetting that you're blaming your actions on others, but it makes me realize your punishment is a fitting one. To make up for your disrespect for our class, you're going to help give back to some other classes."

"What do you mean?"

"I talked with your parents, and we decided you should lose your recess every day for the rest of the month."

"Where will I go during recess?"

"You will help out in other classrooms. There are seventeen school days until Halloween.

You'll visit a different classroom every day and help out however the teacher sees fit."

"Okay," I said. "But what if Myrtle comes back before then? Does that mean my punishment ends?"

"Seventeen days is the deal, and you're going to help out every last one of them."

10
Where's the Blue Clone Trooper?

"**H**ow did school go today?" Dad asked at dinner.

"It was fine," I said.

"He has to help out the other classes for the rest of the month as a punishment," Becky tattled.

"I know, Becky," Dad said. "Mom and I spoke with Mrs. Cliff over the weekend."

"You're going to miss recess for the rest of the month!" Mindy exclaimed.

"I know," I said. "The whole thing is completely lame, too, because Cameron totally set me up to get in trouble."

"You're the only one that can get yourself in trouble," Mom pointed out.

"I shouldn't have picked up Myrtle, but he should have never dared me to do it."

My parents and the girls didn't get it. I had definitely messed up by picking up Myrtle, but Cameron hadn't gotten in any trouble at all, and he had basically bribed me to do it. What kid would turn down thirty dollars for thirty seconds of work?

Later that night, I was playing with my snakes when I realized my Clone Trooper costume hadn't arrived yet. I walked down to the living room, where Mom and Dad were watching television.

"Mom, did my costume come in the mail today?" I asked.

"No, it didn't. It should have come by now."

"Maybe it's late because of the holiday week-end," Dad suggested.

"Can we check to see if it was sent out yet?" I asked.

Mom logged on to the computer and checked to see if the company had sent her a shipping confirmation, but they hadn't. Then she went on the site that she bought it from and sent them an email asking when we should expect the shipment.

I walked into the kitchen and sat at the table with the girls. Their costumes were starting to actually look like lions. Mindy was sewing the tail onto hers. "It's not too late for us to start on a Simba costume," she said.

"If you were Simba, it would be the cutest thing ever!" Becky said.

"I don't want to be the cutest thing ever. I want to be a Clone Trooper. I wish it would get here already. I want to make sure it's the right one."

"You know, if you decided to be Simba, you could be in the contest with us," Becky said.

"What contest?" I asked.

"There's a costume contest at school for all fourth, fifth, and sixth graders. It's at our school on Halloween day," Mindy said.

"I don't think I got anything about it at school," I said.

"It's probably in your backpack. Mindy and I got the notice today. Why don't you ever read anything they hand out?" Becky asked.

I ran to my backpack, and there was a note about the contest. Mrs. Cliff hands out so much garbage each day that I don't read any of it. The note said that there'd be a contest held at my school on Halloween and the winner would win a hundred-dollar gift card to Game Slam.

I don't enter contests because they usually have some sort of work involved, like making a drawing or writing an essay or something, but this one seemed perfect. All I needed was a killer costume, and my Clone Trooper costume would definitely be the best one. I figured I had that gift card in the bag already. I spent the rest of the night on the Game Slam site deciding on what games I would buy after I won.

11
Payback Is a Blast

Wednesday, I lost my first recess, and I loved it! I was sent to Mrs. Cook's class to help organize her library. All the first graders kept coming over and trying to talk with me. They were really fun, and I kind of liked having a break from the rest of my class for a while.

On Thursday, I helped out in Mrs. Floaster's class. She had me clean out the fish tank, which was fine with me because I love animals. It took me so long I was late getting back to class, but Mrs. Cliff didn't seem to mind.

Friday, she sent me to another first-grade class, but the teacher was absent, and the sub didn't know what to do with me. She told me to read to a bunch of first graders for twenty minutes. The kids were so excited to have a fourth grader read to them that I felt like a rock star.

The next week, the punishment got even better when Mrs. Lendal's class had a birthday party for one of the kids in the class, and I had to help hand out cupcakes. I even got to eat one and listen to one of the class parents read a story to the class. It reminded me of when I was little and in first grade. They have it pretty good down there in first grade. They sing, listen to stories, and have none of the stress and pressure a fourth grader has to deal with.

I think Mrs. Cliff started to realize her punishment wasn't having the effect she'd hoped for on Wednesday, when I came back into the class whistling and smiling from ear to ear. I had just come from Mrs. Boudet's class. I had to sharpen about a hundred pencils, and I didn't mind one bit. Mrs. Boudet has this awesome sharpener that's really loud, so she asked me to take it outside. She let me bring her cushioned leather rolling chair. It was a beautiful day out, and I relaxed in the shade, in comfort, while I sharpened the pencils.

"May I talk to you in the hall a moment, Justin?" she asked when I returned.

"Sure!" I said, a little too happy.

We walked into the hall. She took her glasses off and put her hand on her chin. "I'm afraid my punishment isn't teaching you anything. You seem to be having a good time in these classes."

"It's hard work, but I'm learning my lesson," I said.

"What lesson are you learning?"

"I've learned that it's fun to help out," I said, making it up as I went. "I wasn't helping the class out when I dropped Myrtle, and it was a bad feeling. Now that I'm helping other classes, it's a good feeling," I said, unsure if she'd buy it.

"Well, I didn't plan on you enjoying your punishment so much, but if you're learning the positive aspects of giving back, then I guess it's worth it."

"Exactly," I agreed.

12
Nobody Move!

On Friday, I sat at my desk drooling on myself from boredom as Mrs. Cliff taught us about multiplication for the ten thousandth time, when I spotted a dark object dart across the floor. My quick reflexes from taking care of my snakes and hunting for critters in the woods sprang into action.

I immediately snapped out of my haze and pounced on it. I slid under Brett Hayt's desk, banging my head on his chair.

Brett yelled at me, "Get off!"

Mrs. Cliff stood and said, "Justin! What are you up to now?"

I held my hands close together to make sure it didn't get out. It was warm. "I caught Myrtle!" I said proudly. The class erupted and leapt from their seats.

"Everyone stay seated!" Mrs. Cliff instructed, walking over to me and kneeling down. "If this is some kind of trick or prank, you're going to be in hot water," she whispered in a tone that gave me goose bumps.

"I'm not kidding," I said. "It's Myrtle! I caught her!"

"Stand up slowly," she said. "Follow me over the tank."

I did as she said and followed her to the tank. She opened the lid, and I placed the mouse inside. Kids had completely ignored her direction to stay in their seats and crowded around.

"She looks much smaller," May said.

"That's because that's not Myrtle," Cameron said. "That's one of her babies!"

I thought Mrs. Cliff was going to cry. The kids shrieked. Jennifer Goulden ran to her chair and stood on it.

"Get down from that chair this instant," Mrs. Cliff demanded.

"I don't want to be in here," Jennifer said, sounding as though she might cry.

"Everything's fine, Jennifer," Mrs. Cliff assured her.

"No, it's not," Jennifer said, pointing to the floor. There was another small mouse scurrying under one of the desks next to hers. It stopped, and the class immediately fell silent.

Mrs. Cliff put her finger over her lips. "Shhhh."

I jumped on the chair in front of me and hopped onto the desk across from Jenny. "Nobody move," I whispered. "I'll get it."

"Justin," Mrs. Cliff hissed, "get down from there immediately!"

But before I could make my move, Mark launched himself toward the mouse and crashed into Jenny's desk like a gigantic bowling ball. Jenny fell off the desk, knocking me over. We all ended up in a pile on the floor.

When I opened my eyes, the mouse was inches from Jenny's head. "Don't move," I whispered. "It's right above your head."

Jenny shrieked again, startling the mouse. It scurried right toward her and got tangled in her long hair. I couldn't believe what I was seeing! The more it tried to get free, the more it tangled itself in her hair. Jenny sprung to her feet, and the mouse went along for the ride. It hung from her hair, wriggling to get free, like a strange, rodent Christmas tree ornament. All the kids in the class completely freaked out. It sounded as though we were all on a roller coaster.

Mrs. Cliff gently grabbed hold of the mouse and tried to calm Jenny down. It wasn't working. She worked to get the mouse untangled from Jenny's hair, but the more she tried, the more it seemed to get stuck.

"Call the nurse!" Mrs. Cliff shouted.

Simon Freudel ran to the phone and called the nurse, who appeared in seconds with a pair of scissors. She quickly cut the mouse out of Jenny's hair, but she was so focused on Jenny that she dropped it. It hit the floor and scurried off under the bookshelf. An eerie quiet fell over the class, as must happen after any disaster. Everyone was kind of in shock. Jenny broke the silence.

"I hate this class! I'm going to tell the principal!"

13
Think about It

The rest of the day was incredibly weird. The principal sent a sub into the room while they sorted out everything that had happened. An ambulance came to the school and picked up Jenny to take her to the hospital.

On the bus ride home, everyone talked about what happened. I sat with my best friend, Aaron. "What's the deal with you, man?" he asked.

"What do you mean?"

"You're always in some kind of trouble lately."

"I don't cause the trouble. It just kind of finds me."

"Two weeks ago, it was letting the mouse in your class go, and now this. You better watch yourself, or you're going to end up in real trouble."

"I didn't do anything!" I insisted.

"I don't know," he said. "Just try to be careful. Halloween is in less than two weeks, and I need someone to go trick-or-treating with."

"We're going to go together," I reminded him.

"Only if your parents let you! If you keep this up, I'll be going by myself. Try to be a little more careful."

It was as if Aaron knew something I didn't, because when I got home, Mom and Dad sat me down at the kitchen table, and Mom said, "I don't know what's gotten into you, but if it keeps up, we're not going to be able to let you go trick-or-treating this year."

"That's not fair!" I said.

"Justin," Dad said, "in the past few weeks, you've gotten in trouble for leaving the tops off your snake tanks, letting the class mouse go, and almost killing a girl in your class. I think what your mother is saying is quite fair."

"I didn't almost kill Jenny today. If anything, I was a hero. She was terrified, and I was trying to help her. Mark's the one who crashed into her desk and knocked us all down."

"But you're forgetting that there's a teacher in the class. It wasn't your place to try and catch the mouse unless she asked you to."

"She wasn't going to catch the mouse! I had to help."

"We're not talking about it anymore. If we get another call or a note from your school, you're not going trick-or-treating. I suggest you keep your nose out of trouble," Dad warned.

It was totally unfair, but what could I do? I was getting the blame, again, and there wasn't anything I could do about it. I marched toward my room, making sure they could tell how angry

I was. Slamming the door was probably pushing my luck.

"Lose that attitude," Mom called.

I opened my bedroom door and found Becky and Mindy were sitting on my bed, grinning.

"What do you two want?" I asked.

"We have a proposition for you," Mindy said.

"I'm not interested."

"You didn't hear what we have to say," Becky countered.

"Doesn't matter. I'm not interested."

"You've managed to get yourself in a lot of trouble, and we're offering a way out," Becky said.

"Go on," I said.

"We're nearing completion of our awesome lion costumes. But without a Simba, we're really just two lions," Mindy said.

"Sure, we could simply carry a Simba stuffed animal, and everyone would know who we are, but having a real-life Simba would be way better," Becky added.

"I already told you guys that I'm going to be a Clone Trooper."

"Think about how cute you'd look as Simba," Mindy continued. "I don't care how much trouble you get yourself into, Mom will think you're the most adorable thing in the world."

"Not interested," I said. "Now if you girls will excuse me, I've had a long day."

"Think about it," Becky said.

"Already did!" I said.

14
Calamity

The next day was Friday the nineteenth. Mrs. Cliff seemed a bit defeated. She must have gotten in a lot of trouble because of the Jenny situation. Jenny was absent. The principal came to our class right after the announcements and sat us all down.

"We have had a lot of dangerous behavior in this class recently, and I expect it to stop at once," she said. "As you all know, a pregnant mouse named Myrtle was released from her tank a couple of weeks ago." She shot me a look.

"It appears that Myrtle has since given birth to a litter of baby mice and they're beginning to explore their surroundings. The average number of babies in a litter is about twelve. So it appears that we have possibly a dozen mice loose in our school."

Mark clapped, which was very awkward because no one else did. The principal gave him a look and said, "I don't understand why you would clap for that, Mark, but it demonstrates the importance of my little chat. This is not a good thing. I am very concerned for everyone's safety, including the mice, and so is Mrs. Cliff. The mice don't pose any harm as long as we leave them alone. I've instructed the custodians to set safe traps in your class at night, and I'm quite certain we'll catch them. If you see any mice during the day, you are to alert Mrs. Cliff immediately and stay away from them. Are there any questions?"

She realized immediately that she shouldn't have opened it up to questions because almost every hand went up. We spent the next forty minutes answering every what-if question the class could think of. It seemed to go on forever.

After the principal left, Mrs. Cliff explained that she had convinced her to allow us to keep the mice for observation as long as we were extremely careful with the tank. Mrs. Cliff had even bought a new tank with a lid that had a latch on the top to make sure the mice couldn't get out.

"No one is to go near this tank unless instructed by me, and no one may open the lid under any circumstance," she ordered.

The rest of the day was completely boring. I couldn't wait to get home for the weekend. At the end of the day, Mrs. Cliff announced, "We are not going to let the series of unfortunate events ruin our study of mammals. We will continue to study the baby mouse we caught yesterday."

You mean the mouse I caught yesterday, I thought.

"I selected a name from the name jar earlier today, and Cameron was selected. I called his parents, and they will be in before the end of the day to take our new mouse home for the weekend. Every weekend for the next few weeks, a different member of the class will be chosen to take our tank home."

May raised her hand. "What if we don't want to?"

"It's voluntary. If you don't want to, I'll pick another name. I told Cameron earlier today, and he agreed to take it for the weekend."

I couldn't believe it. Cameron didn't deserve to take the mouse home for the weekend. I was clearly the only one in the class with any understanding of animals.

Then Mrs. Cliff said, "I've also named our newest mouse. Her name is Calamity. Does anyone know what a calamity is?"

No one raised a hand to answer.

"A calamity is an event that causes great and often sudden damage or distress. Yesterday was a calamity, and so that's what we will call her."

15
The Best Halloween Ever

All weekend I thought about how lucky Cameron was that he had gotten to take Calamity home. I played with Mr. Squeeze and Stanky most of the time because I was grounded. Mom and Dad wouldn't even let me go to my soccer game on Saturday. My coach called after the game to tell me how disappointed he was in me, and that I'd better get my act together. It felt as though everyone I knew was mad at me.

The next week things were pretty calm at school. Jenny returned on Monday, and you couldn't even tell she'd had a patch of hair cut out. But the rest of the kids and Mrs. Cliff treated her as if she'd survived a plane crash. No one seemed to remember that I'd gotten knocked off a desk trying to save her, and that I was the one who'd caught Calamity in the first place.

The custodians safely caught three more baby mice, for a total of four babies in the tank. They were super cute. Mrs. Cliff named them Miracle, Marvel, and Wonder.

I continued to visit classes during recess and realized how much better the rest of the school had it. The other classes seemed like so much fun compared to Mrs. Cliff's class. Even Mrs. Sholden, who people say is the meanest teacher in the school, seemed like a sweetheart compared to Mrs. Cliff.

On Friday, I had to help out in Mrs. Fiesta's class, which I was psyched about because she's the coolest teacher in the whole school and most of my friends are in her class. I walked in and they were sitting in a circle on the floor.

"Hi, Justin," she said. "I have a bunch of books on the back table that need to be sorted by reading level. Thank you for your help."

"Okay," I said, sitting in a chair at the table.

"So, class," she continued, "our Halloween party is almost set. We only have the issue of food to decide. The food committee is going to give a few choices, and then we'll take a vote. Remember, you can only vote once."

Two girls with clipboards stood up, and one of them said, "Okay, we've narrowed the food down to pizza, hot dogs, or burgers."

"How many people want pizza?" the second girl asked.

I could hardly believe my ears. The girl gave the class the other choices and tallied the votes.

"So that's decided," Mrs. Fiesta said. "We'll have pizza on Halloween, so don't bother bringing a lunch from home. We've already decided that we'll have cupcakes, provided by Ted's parents' bakery, and I'll have a bunch of fun games for us to play, along with the gross-out boxes I told you about."

Mrs. Cliff's punishment was finally working on me. It was torture listening to all the
amazing things Mrs. Fiesta's class was doing for
Halloween.

When it was time to return to class, Mrs.
Fiesta said, "Thank you, Justin, you may return
to class now."

"No thanks," I said. "I'll stay."

"You can't stay. Mrs. Cliff will be expecting
you."

"Please," I pleaded. "Let me stay. I'll do
anything."

It didn't work. She sent me back. As I was
walking out the door, they were deciding on
what spooky Halloween music they'd use for the
party. When I got back to Mrs. Cliff's room, they
were reading silently.

I sat down at my desk and took out the same
book I'd been reading since the first day of school.
Mrs. Cliff encouraged me to choose something
else just about every day, but I wouldn't. I usually

just looked at the pictures, and sometimes just daydreamed and pretended to be reading.

I was deep in a daydream, and my eyes were about to close, when I heard Mrs. Cliff say, "Justin, please come over to my desk."

Here we go, I thought. *What now?*

16
Can I Trust You?

"Justin, I wanted to tell you that you've done a very good job this week keeping out of trouble," Mrs. Cliff said.

"Thanks, but I shouldn't have been in trouble in the first place because Cameron—" I tried to explain.

"Let's not relive the past," she said. "While you were out at Mrs. Fiesta's class, I selected the person who'll be taking care of the mice over the weekend. Your name was selected, and against my better judgment, I'm going to let you take care of them for the weekend. This is a chance to redeem yourself. Can I trust you with this responsibility?"

"Yes, ma'am," I said confidently. Mrs. Cliff surprised me. I couldn't believe she would send the mice home with me after all that happened.

My parents picked me up after school, and we carried the tank out to the parking lot.

"This is a big responsibility," Mom said once we were in the car.

"Please don't make us regret this decision," Dad said.

"I won't. This is going to be a piece of cake. I take care of mice all the time," I reminded them.

"You feed mice to your snakes," Dad said. "There's a difference."

17
Don't Tell Mom and Dad

Saturday, I asked Mom and Dad if Aaron could sleep over. They agreed since I'd had a good week at school and I'd been grounded the two weekends before. Aaron came over around four, and we played outside until dark. I was so glad that Mindy and Becky were putting the finishing touches on their costumes because if they weren't, they would have been driving us crazy. Instead, it was as if they weren't even home.

Mom said we could play with the snakes as long as we kept the mouse tank safely on my desk and the lid secure. Aaron's parents don't let him have any pets, so he loves playing with the snakes when he comes over.

"Your sisters' costumes are pretty amazing," Aaron said, draping Mr. Squeeze over his shoulders. "You still haven't told me what you're going to be for Halloween."

"I'm not being a part of their costume this year," I said, "if that's what you're wondering. I'm going to be something cool enough that I think I might win that contest at school."

"What is it?" he asked.

"I'm not saying. It should have come in the mail weeks ago. My mom's been trying to track down the shipment, but it seems to be lost in the mail or something."

"I'm going to be a zombie," Aaron said. "It's going to be awesome. You're going to come home on the bus to my house so we can trick-or-treat immediately after school, right?"

"That's the plan," I said, putting Stanky back in his tank.

My dad knocked on the door and came in. "You guys can stay up until about ten, and then you have to hit the hay. Aaron's parents are picking him up bright and early tomorrow morning."

"We will, Dad."

Aaron and I played video games for a while, ate pizza in my room, and then put on *Night of the Deadsies 7.* The movie was about an hour too long, and the second half was just boring and ridiculous. We must have both fallen asleep because the next thing I knew, Mom was calling from downstairs that Aaron's parents had arrived. Aaron quickly gathered up his things and we went downstairs.

I grabbed a cup of orange juice from the fridge and went back up to my room to play video games. Becky walked in a few minutes later and sat at my desk.

"Can I use your computer?" she asked. "Mine's acting funny."

"Sure."

She opened my computer and then said, "Didn't you say there were four mice in that tank?"

"Yeah, why?"

"Because I only see three."

"The fourth one is probably hiding behind something," I assured her.

"I don't think so. I think there are only three in there."

My heart immediately beat triple time. I ran to my closet. Mr. Squeeze wasn't in his tank. Aaron and I must have fallen asleep before we could lock him back up.

Becky appeared next to me. "No way!" she said, looking at the empty tank. "You left your snake out overnight!"

"Please, Becky," I begged. "Don't tell Mom and Dad. Give me a minute to find him and figure this out."

"Don't tell Mom and Dad what?" Mom said from outside the closet.

18
Calamity's Calamity

"**H**ow could you be so irresponsible?" Mom asked after I explained that Mr. Squeeze was missing.

"It wasn't my fault," I said. "I put Stanky back in his tank while we were watching the movie. Aaron must have forgotten to put Mr. Squeeze back in his tank."

"I can't believe you're trying to blame this on your friend!"

"Seriously," Becky said, grinning. "You're messed up."

"Becky!" Mom said. "Go get your father."

"You got it, Mom. Should I tell him that one of the mice is missing too?" she asked, knowing this would set Mom off.

"Excuse me?" Mom said.

"He had four mice on Friday, and now there are only three," Becky said.

"Go get your father, *please*," Mom said, looking as if she might explode.

I tried to look as cute as I could, given the situation, but even I knew there wasn't enough cute in the world to get me out of this one.

It took me about fifteen minutes to find Mr. Squeeze. He was wrapped around the heater under my desk. It took me a few minutes to untangle him. Mom, Dad, and the girls stood nervously waiting for me to get him free. They were all thinking what I already knew: Mr. Squeeze had eaten the missing mouse.

When I finally got him free, Becky said, "Is that lump in his belly..."

"Yep," I said. "That's Calamity."

The rest of the day was pretty quiet at my house. Mom and Dad didn't say much to me about it. I think they were shocked and confused about how to explain it to Mrs. Cliff.

I woke Monday morning and was surprised by how numb I felt. It was as if all the fear had somehow been scared right out of me. Dad carried the tank with the three mice out to the car, and I followed. Mom and the girls were already in the car. I buckled into my spot in the middle between the girls. It was so quiet it was painful.

I had to break the silence, and the only thing I could think to say was, "So, do you think my costume will come today?"

19
You Win

When my parents and I told Mrs. Cliff what happened to Calamity, she cried. When she told the rest of the class later that morning, they cried. I had fed about a hundred mice to my snakes, but somehow, I felt like crying too. The principal sent the counselor to our class to talk to the kids about death, which I thought was a little over the top.

The rest of the day went by really slow. I felt terrible. I hadn't meant for the mouse to get eaten, but I certainly was getting blamed for it. No one in the class would talk to me.

Tuesday, things didn't get any better. That night, Mom came into my room and sat on my bed next to me. "Justin, your costume came the other day in the mail, but I'm afraid you can't wear it tomorrow."

"I know," I said. "Can I at least see it?"

"No," she said. "I'll hold on to it for you for next year."

"That's fair," I said. "I'm sorry I've caused so much trouble lately."

"I know you are. I also know it hasn't all been your fault, but you need to learn to be more careful so you don't get yourself into these situations."

"Can I go trick-or-treating with Aaron tomorrow?"

"I'm afraid not."

"All right," I said. I didn't like it, but my fate was sealed.

Mom walked out, and Becky and Mindy walked in. Mindy held out a Simba costume.

"You win," I said. "I'll be Simba."

20
Simba, the Halloween Monster

Halloween in Mrs. Cliff's class wasn't as bad as I thought. Sure I was dressed like Simba, but she brought in a bunch of snacks and even played spooky Halloween music as we all shared our research reports. I shared my report on werewolves and listened to reports on vampires, zombies, and Frankenstein. When they were all over, I felt pretty sorry for vampires, zombies, werewolves, and every other kind of monster because I knew how they felt—in my class, I was the worst monster of them all.

The only positive was that Becky, Mindy, and I won the best costume award, even though no one in my class voted for us. The girls were so excited they let me keep the hundred-dollar gift card to Game Slam we'd won.

Instead of trick-or-treating after school with Aaron like I planned, I spent the rest of the day dressed as Simba from the Lion King handing out candy to other kids. It was a perfectly awful end to a perfectly awful Halloween. Hopefully I'll still fit into my Clone Trooper costume next Halloween.

50876176R00058

Made in the USA
Charleston, SC
10 January 2016